Turtle Beach

Written by Barbara A Arrindell

Illustrated by Zavian Archibald

Collins

Happy birthday!

Anaïs ran ahead of her parents. Today was special. It was her seventh birthday.

Dad had decided that she was old enough to go to a restaurant for dinner. She couldn't believe her luck!

"Slow down, Anaïs," Dad called. He hoped that this was a birthday celebration she would always remember.

Anaïs waited at the restaurant entrance, trying hard to be patient. The sand under her feet was slipping into her sandals. She giggled as she tried to shake it out of one sandal and even more slipped into the other.

Unspoilt land

Mom told her that the winding road they had driven on had only just been built. The builders had discovered many animals.

Thousands of monkeys lived in the trees, and deer and peacocks hid in the bushes.

Anaïs hoped to see some of the amazing wildlife. She knew that some of the animals were curious when they saw people, while others ran away.

5

The seashore

A tall man greeted them. "Welcome to Turtle
Beach Restaurant."

Mom told him that it was Anaïs's birthday,
and he smiled.

"Since it's your birthday, you can choose your table,
young lady."

Anaïs wanted to sit as close to the seashore as possible.
She couldn't wait to look out to sea and hear
the waves as they gently came ashore.

Anaïs noticed two large floodlights on the beach. They lit up the seashore and two people who were walking in the distance. Maybe after dinner, they could walk on the beach too.

Guava smoothies

"May I please have a guava smoothie?" she asked.

Then she looked at the menu and felt confused. There were so many things to choose from.

Dad suggested they order three different meals and share them. That meant that Anaïs could try three new things. She was delighted!

Anaïs looked back at the water. It was so beautiful.

Then she saw something that scared her. It looked like a big shiny thing slithering over the sand. Anaïs had no idea what it was, but the strange creature was coming towards the restaurant. A tingling started in her tummy.

Baby turtles

Within seconds, the restaurant became very quiet. Other people had seen what Anaïs was looking at, and they didn't know what to do.

Then a clear voice shouted, "Turn off all the lights!"

"Those are baby turtles that have just hatched,"
explained the voice. "They think that the floodlights
are the moonlight, so they are coming up the beach
instead of going towards the water."

Lights out

Quickly, the lights were turned off. The bright
full moon made it possible to still see the turtles.
Together, they had looked like a giant sea creature,
but now Anaïs saw that there were more than
100 tiny turtles. She almost cried with excitement.

Anaïs wondered where their parents were. Don't all
babies need adults to protect them?

When the lights went off, the turtles stopped suddenly.
For more than a minute, not one of them moved.

"What has happened to them?" Anaïs cried.

Then, as suddenly as they had stopped, they all turned around. It was magical to be there; to see this happening. With the moon in front of them, an army of baby turtles made their way towards the sea.

Everyone in the restaurant clapped. Some even cried as they realised what had just happened. By turning off a light, they had saved the lives of the baby turtles.

Helping

Everyone in the restaurant had stood up to watch the turtles. Some people wanted to rush out and help.

The lady said that they shouldn't. She explained that the baby turtles knew what to do. "Picking up the turtles can harm them," she explained. "We need to let them follow the moonlight back to the sea. A few might need a hand." Once most of the turtles were safely in the water, she said she would check that none were trapped.

As she walked past Anaïs's table, the lady saw
the birthday balloons. She also saw how excited
Anaïs was.

"Would you like to help?" she asked Anaïs.

Anaïs's parents said that she could go. Mom knew
the lady very well.

As they walked along the beach, they saved a few turtles that hadn't made it to the water. One had been caught in a cup. Another couldn't free itself from a plastic bag.

Anaïs realised that the garbage had almost killed the baby turtles. From now on, she was going to remind everyone that they shouldn't litter.

Good luck, little ones

The babies were gently placed in the water.
They swam away happily. The lady was right!
They really did know what to do.

Anaïs started clapping. She was so happy that they
had all made it to the water.

Walking back to the restaurant, the lady explained that the turtles were leatherbacks. "They usually hatch between September and October," she said. "In 13 or 14 years, when you are 21, those babies will come back here to lay their eggs."

Anaïs realised that the turtles shared the same birthday as her. "Maybe," she thought, "just maybe, I'll get to see my new friends again, if I come back to Turtle Beach to celebrate my 21st birthday."

Baby turtles follow light

Baby turtles walk towards the first light they see.

They might walk towards a bright white light on a lamppost or building.

To stay alive, they need to walk towards the sea.

Ideas for reading

Written by Christine Whitney
Primary Literacy Consultant

Reading objectives:
- discuss the sequence of events in books
- make inferences on the basis of what is being said and done
- predict what might happen on the basis of what has been read so far

Spoken language objectives:
- ask relevant questions
- speculate, imagine and explore ideas through talk
- participate in discussions

Curriculum links: Science – children should use the local environment throughout the year to explore and answer questions about animals in their habitat;
Writing – write narratives about personal experiences and those of others, write for different purposes

Word count: 904

Interest words: unspoilt land, hatch, leatherbacks

Resources: paper and pencils, fruit to make a smoothie with – if possible, use guava as mentioned in the story

Build a context for reading

- Ask children to tell each other what they know about turtles. Do they know any stories about turtles?

- Read the blurb on the back cover. Ask children to tell the group what they know about the start of a baby turtle's life. Where would they normally hatch?

- Cover the text and look at the illustration of Anaïs arriving at the restaurant on pp2–3. Ask children to talk about what Anaïs might be thinking as she waits for her parents to catch up. Children could write their ideas in a thought bubble.

Understand and apply reading strategies

- Read pp4–5. Ask children what animals had been discovered as the builders built the road to the restaurant.